THE BROTHERS GRUESOME

For Francesca, Dagmar and Gia

Walter Lorraine *wn* Books

First American edition 2000
Originally published in Australia as an Angus&Robertson book by
HarperCollinsPublishers Pty Limited.
http://www.harpercollins.com.au

Library of Congress Cataloging-in-Publication Data:
Elgar, Susan.
The brothers gruesome / written by Susan Elgar :
illustrated by Drahos Zak.
p.   cm.
Summary: Three horrible and hungry brothers eat everything in their path,
including their mother, the bath, animals, and gardens, until they meet
something even bigger, hungrier, and hairier than they are.
ISBN 0–618–00515–3
[1. Brothers Fiction. 2. Greed Fiction. 3. Monsters Fiction.
4. Stories in rhyme.] I. Zak, Drahos, ill. II. Title.
PZ8.3.E42Br 1999
[E] – dc21
99–20057
CTP

Printed by Sino Publishing House Pty Ltd., Hong Kong.

10 9 8 7 6 5 4 3 2 1

Drahos Zak

THE BROTHERS GRUESOME

story by
Susan Elgar

Houghton Mifflin Company, Boston 2000

Walter Lorraine Books

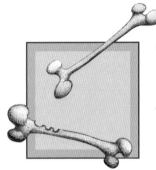 Three brothers there were, a gruesome threesome,

And not only ugly, but wicked and fearsome.

They were awfully cruel and terribly horrid,

And each of them had giant warts on his forehead.

Three ugly brothers so disgusting and rotten,

Theirs is a tale that cannot be forgotten.

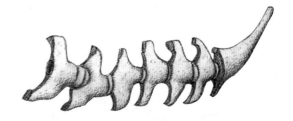

 In the town of their birth they were loathed and feared,

But in the depths of hell they were worshiped and cheered.

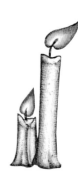

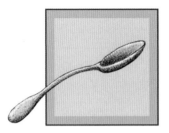 These brothers were born one wild, windy night,

So incredibly ugly even their mother took fright.

 And once they arrived they demanded food,

Their manners – what manners? – they were monstrously rude!

 When their mother no longer could fill up their bellies,

They gobbled her up in her raincoat and wellies.

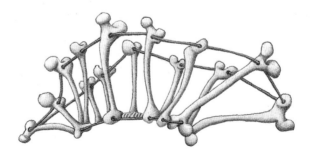

They greedily munched their way through the house,

Stuffing everything in – even the tiniest mouse!

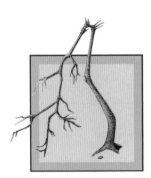

Away they went thinking of all they'd devour,

Not caring a bit be it sweet or sour.

The terrified townsfolk ran away from these cannibals,

And so, one by one, the brothers devoured the animals!

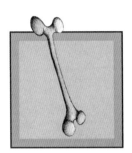

They dug up the rocks and uprooted the trees,

They ate all the gardens and gulped all the bees.

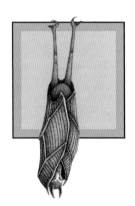

They ate every grain of last season's crop,

Drank up the river to the very last drop.

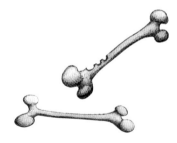

 To the three ugly brothers it did not matter,

That every day they grew bigger and fatter.

They thought of themselves as the biggest, the best,

Not stopping a moment to think of the rest.

Off they stomped, singing, "We're kings of the area,"

But they never counted on something

bigger,
hungrier, and
hairier!